Dear Parents:

Congratulations! Your child is taking the first steps on an exciting journey. The destination? Independent reading!

STEP INTO READING® will help your child get there. The program offers five steps to reading success. Each step includes fun stories and colorful art or photographs. In addition to original fiction and books with favorite characters, there are Step into Reading Non-Fiction Readers, Phonics Readers and Boxed Sets, Sticker Readers, and Comic Readers—a complete literacy program with something to interest every child.

Learning to Read, Step by Step!

Ready to Read   Preschool–Kindergarten
• big type and easy words • rhyme and rhythm • picture clues
For children who know the alphabet and are eager to begin reading.

Reading with Help   Preschool–Grade 1
• basic vocabulary • short sentences • simple stories
For children who recognize familiar words and sound out new words with help.

Reading on Your Own   Grades 1–3
• engaging characters • easy-to-follow plots • popular topics
For children who are ready to read on their own.

Reading Paragraphs   Grades 2–3
• challenging vocabulary • short paragraphs • exciting stories
For newly independent readers who read simple sentences with confidence.

Ready for Chapters   Grades 2–4
• chapters • longer paragraphs • full-color art
For children who want to take the plunge into chapter books but still like colorful pictures.

STEP INTO READING® is designed to give every child a successful reading experience. The grade levels are only guides; children will progress through the steps at their own speed, developing confidence in their reading.

Remember, a lifetime love of reading starts with a single step!

Published in the United States by Random House Children's Books, a division of Penguin Random House LLC, 1745 Broadway, New York, NY 10019, and in Canada by Penguin Random House Canada Limited, Toronto.

Step into Reading, Random House, and the Random House colophon are registered trademarks of Penguin Random House LLC.

Visit us on the Web!
StepIntoReading.com
randomhousekids.com

Educators and librarians, for a variety of teaching tools, visit us at
RHTeachersLibrarians.com

ISBN 978-0-399-55483-4 (trade) — ISBN 978-0-399-55484-1 (lib. bdg.) —
ISBN 978-0-399-55485-8 (ebook)

Printed in the United States of America

10 9 8 7 6 5 4 3 2

MAX

Max is one lucky dog.
He lives in New York City
in an apartment building
filled with his pals.

Max loves his owner, Katie,

and waits all day

for her to come home.

DUKE

Duke was adopted
from the pound.
He is Max's new brother.

Duke is excited about his new home,
but Max isn't ready to share.

GIDGET

Gidget loves Max.

She is the sweetest Pomeranian,

but don't let her squeaky voice

...ffy fur fool you.

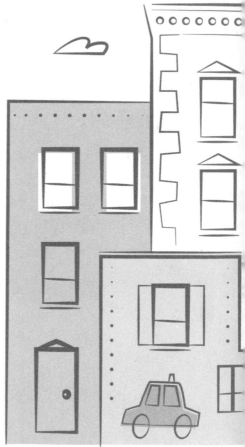

Gidget would go anywhere

or do anything to save Max.

one fussy feline.
Chloe can't be bothered,
unless you have food.

Max is one of her best friends,
even though he's a dog.

MEL

Mel is a friendly pug,
but not when it comes
to squirrels.

He thinks squirrels are
going to take over the world!
Mel chases and barks at them
every chance he gets.

BUDDY

Buddy is short,
long, and awesome.
Mel and Buddy are
best friends.

Buddy and Mel go a long way
to help their pal Max.

NORMAN

Norman is always lost.
This guinea pig travels through
the building's air vents,
looking for his home.

Somehow, he always ends up

at Max's house.

LEONARD

Leonard looks like
a pretty posh poodle.
But Leonard turns up the volume
and becomes a heavy-metal mutt
after his owner leaves.

POPS

Even though Pops needs
a doggie wheelchair,
this old basset hound gets around.
He knows the city like he knows
the back of his paw.

When Max goes missing,
Pops leads his friends
on the search to find him.

SNOWBALL

Snowball is one tough bunny.
Abandoned by his owner,
Snowball vowed revenge
on all humans.

He is the leader
of the Flushed Pets.
These abandoned pets
live in the sewers beneath
New York City.

**LIBERATED FOREVER,
DOMESTICATED NEVER!**

This cat has a bad attitude!
Ozone and his gang rule
the alleys and fight dirty.

They don't like intruders
on their territory.

TATTOO

This tough potbellied pig
got inked by his owners.
They practiced drawing
their tattoos on him.
Now Tattoo works for Snowball
as his faithful second-in-command.

BEARDED DRAGON

Bearded Dragon is
a cold-blooded lizard.

He loves to drive cars,
even though he doesn't know how.

He is crazy at the wheel!

Max and his friends
and the Flushed Pets
are all special
and need lots of love.